F. J. Hughes

Harmonies Of Tones And Colours Developed by Evolution

F. J. Hughes

Harmonies Of Tones And Colours Developed by Evolution

ISBN/EAN: 9783337471200

Printed in Europe, USA, Canada, Australia, Japan

Cover: Foto ©Andreas Hilbeck / pixelio.de

More available books at **www.hansebooks.com**

HARMONIES

OF

TONES AND COLOURS

Developed by Evolution

BY F. J. HUGHES

"Thy testimonies are wonderful."—PSALM cxix. 129.

"Search the Scriptures . . . they are they which testify of Me" (*Revised Version*—"these are they which bear witness of Me").—JOHN v. 39.

"For I doubt not through the ages one increasing purpose runs,
And the thoughts of men are wider with the process of the suns."—*Tennyson.*

London:
MARCUS WARD & CO., 67 & 68, CHANDOS STREET
AND AT BELFAST AND NEW YORK
MDCCCLXXXIII.

Dedication.

TO a beloved circle of relatives and friends, and also with the deepest respect to those searchers after truth who, without implicit trust in their own finite powers, take delight in tracing the deep laws of the Almighty as typified in His word, and embodied in the beautiful work of Nature.

CONTENTS.

INTRODUCTION.

PART I.

CHAPTER I.

CHAPTER II.

CHAPTER III.

PART II.

CHAPTER IV.—DIAGRAM I.

CHAPTER V.—DIAGRAM II.

CHAPTER VI.—DIAGRAM III.

CHAPTER VII.—DIAGRAM IV.

·CHAPTER VIII.—DIAGRAM V.

CHAPTER IX.—DIAGRAM VI.

CONCLUSION.

APPENDIX.

EXTRACTS FROM LETTERS ADDRESSED TO F. J. HUGHES BY DR. GAUNTLETT.

FRAGMENTS FROM LAST NOTE-BOOK OF DR. GAUNTLETT.

INTRODUCTION.

"The words of the Lord are pure words: as silver tried in a furnace of earth, purified seven times."—PSA. xii. 6.

"Life, presence everywhere sublimely vast,
And endless for the future as the past."
M. F. Tupper.

THE following scheme endeavours to show that the development of the musical gamut and the colours of the rainbow are regulated by the same laws. I wish it to be clearly understood that I have gained the evolutions from the mysterious type of Life—a golden thread running throughout the Scriptures, from the first chapter of Genesis to the last of Revelation;—life developing around us and within us from the Almighty, who is its Eternal Fountain. My youthful impressions included the belief that the views of Dr. Darwin, my great-uncle, contradicted the teaching of the Scriptures, and I therefore avoided them altogether. Having endeavoured for years to gain correctly the laws which develope Evolution, I suddenly discovered that I was working from Scripture on the same foundation which he had found in Creation; and as Creation and Revelation proceed from the same Author, I knew that they could not contradict each other. It is considered by many that my cousin, Charles Darwin, gained his first ideas of Evolution from his grandfather's works; but I know from himself that he was ignorant of them, and that his theory of Evolution was arrived at by his close experiments and observations of the laws of creation alone. Only a few months since, after reading his work on "the Movements of Plants," published in 1881, and wishing to be certain that I had not an incorrect belief, I asked the following question—"Did you gain your views on Evolution by your wonderfully acute observations, ignorant of your grandfather's ideas?" The reply was, that he had done so entirely from his own observations.

It is my firm belief that, if a powerful intellect takes up the radical idea contained in the following pages, it will be found to be the directing force or general key-note which will gradually disentangle intricacies in all the natural

sciences, and link, by the same mode of physical evolution, the past, the present, and the future.

I enter upon the subject with the deepest sense of my own inability to do justice in any measure to the grandeur of the topic; but I trust that my remarks may prove suggestive to others of far higher truths. They are the result of the leisure hours of nearly fifty years, during which the conviction has ever deepened, that "philosophy of the natural kind does but push man's ignorance farther back," and that, in the concluding words of Sir John Lubbock's inaugural address to the British Association at York in 1881, "the great lesson which Science teaches is, how little we yet know, and how much we have still to learn."

If health is still granted to me, and if an interest is created on the subject of these pages, I shall endeavour to explain by what means I gained the laws here described, and to enter upon the development of numbers as showing the stream of time ever falling into infinity, and gliding onwards; also the sevens in creation, with several other branches of the subject which are here untouched, or but briefly alluded to. It is my earnest desire that all may be closely examined. Indifference will grieve me, but even severe criticism will afford me pleasure, as proving that the subject is considered worthy of investigation.

The publication of this work has been unavoidably delayed for a year, and I now quote briefly from an address of Dr. C. W. Siemens, during the late meeting of the British Association at Southampton, as reported in the *Times.* I have strictly endeavoured to make my investigations according to his views of combining scientific knowledge with practical utility.

"The time was when Science was cultivated only by the few, who looked upon its application to the arts and manufactures as almost beneath their consideration: this they were content to leave in the hands of others, who, with only commercial aims in view, did not aspire to further the objects of Science for its own sake, but thought only of benefiting by its teachings. Progress could not be rapid under this condition of things, because the man of pure science rarely pursued his inquiry beyond the mere enunciation of a physical or chemical principle, while the simple practitioner was at a loss how to harmonise the new knowledge with the stock of information which formed his mental capital in trade. The advancement of the last fifty years has, I venture to submit, rendered theory and practice so interdependent, that an intimate union between them is a matter of absolute necessity for our future progress." "It is to the man of science, who also gives attention to practical questions, and to the practitioner, who devotes part of his time to the prosecution of strictly scientific investigation, that we owe the rapid progress of the present day, both merging more and more into one class, that of pioneers in the domain of Nature." "These considerations may serve to show that, although we see the men of both abstract and applied science group themselves

in minor bodies for the better prosecution of special objects, the points of contact between the different branches of knowledge are ever multiplying, all tending to form part of a mighty tree—the tree of modern science." "In this short word *energy* we find all the efforts in Nature—energy is life in action." "We shall thus find that in the great workshop of Nature there are no lines of demarcation to be drawn between the most exalted speculation and commonplace practice, and that all knowledge must lead up to one great result, that of an intelligent recognition of the Creator through His works."

F. J. HUGHES.

HEDWYN LODGE,
SANDOWN, ISLE OF WIGHT,
April, 1883.

PART I.

CHAPTER I.

GENERAL REMARKS ON HARMONIES OF TONES AND COLOURS.

" On crazy fabrics ill-timed cost bestowed
No purpose answers, when discretion bids
To pull them down, and wait a season fit
To build anew."

ALTHOUGH I am confident that the foundation on which I have been building is firm, and will never fail, I also feel that there are probably errors in raising the superstructure. "Truthful deductions must ultimately harmonise; like light, they will shine by their own effulgence." "If, however, we determine that we will not receive any truth against which objections can be raised, we shall remain in a state of universal scepticism, for against truths of every description objections have been and may be suggested." Appearances are often contrary to facts— "the straight stick looks crooked in the tide." And the question has always to be decided, whether the objections neutralise the positive evidences in favour of the truth of any assertion.

It seems desirable that I should briefly state my entire ignorance of natural science, and that what I do know has been gained without technical knowledge, with the determination that imagination should not interfere with strict investigation.

I had for a long time studied the development of the harmonies of colour, and believed that I had gained them correctly ; but I saw no way of proving this. The thought occurred—Why not test the laws in musical harmonies ? I wrote down the development of the seven major keys of the white notes in keyed instruments. I was perplexed by the movement as of "to and fro," but the development of numbers explained this point, and I found that the method of development in colours, tones, and numbers agreed. I remembered the keys with sharps, but had forgotten that B♭ belonged to the key of F, and here I thought that the laws failed. But I found by reference that all were correct, the eighth being the first of a higher series, the laws having enabled me to distinguish between flats and sharps,

whether veering round, or advancing and retreating in musical clef. I next tried the major keys which develope flats, and I thought that G♭ would develope a perfect harmony, but found that it must be F♯, and that in this one harmony E♭ must be used in place of F♮; on reference, I found that thus the twelve keys developed correctly in succession, the thirteenth being the octave, or first of a higher series.

I had forgotten all the minor keys, except that A is the relative minor of C major; but although I had only faint hopes of success, I determined to try, and I gained the twelve keys correctly, with the thirteenth octave. I found also that E♭ was usually printed as a minor key-note, Nature's laws having shown that it must be D♯.

In a few remarks on "Tones and Colours," inserted in the *Athenæum* of February 24, 1877, I alluded to the great loss I had sustained by the sudden death of Dr. Gauntlett. I often retrace with grateful remembrance the kind manner in which he examined this scheme when it was but crude and imperfect; with a very capacious intellect, he had a warm and generous heart, causing him to think over with candour any new ideas placed before him. He was of the greatest use to me, by corroborating the points which I had gained. I remarked to him one day, "I find that, of the double tones, F♯ is a key-note and G♭ a root." He replied, "You must have a right foundation to work upon, or you would never have ascertained the necessity of the two poles; you have gained the double tones correctly, and the development of harmonies without limit. On this point I have always felt the failure of the laws followed by the musician."

I add quotations from the first letter I received from him. "I have read the MS., and there are some very curious coincidences—exceedingly so—here and there. Whether it will clear out into a demonstrable system, I cannot say at present. If we can get our harmonical start, I think all will come out plainly, for there is so much that is consistent in sequence. There has been nothing at all like it at present, and some of it squares singularly with the old Greek notions." "I am more than half a disciple of your theory of the six tones, and am inclined to imagine that it would do away with much complication, and keep the mind bent on a smaller circle. We can only see things in patches, and hear in trinities, and every single sound is a trinity."

There is amazing grandeur, united with simplicity, in the working of Nature's laws in the development of harmonies of sound, so that the smallest conceivable point has its complementary and corresponding gradation, which renders it capable of development into its peculiar harmony, causing the "multequivalency of harmonies" in endless variety, whether veering round, to and fro, ascending or descending, or advancing and retiring in musical clef.

I also wish to explain that I have, in several instances, interwoven sentences from different authors, and other remarks of the late Dr. Gauntlett; but as they are not *verbatim*, they are not always noticed as quotations.

I am aware that I have entered upon many points well known to musicians; as I have had to learn, so I wished to explain to those who have not studied the science. There are many interesting points on which I have not entered. I ask any who look into the subject to suspend their judgment until they have closely examined it from beginning to end.

CHAPTER II.

THE METHOD OF DEVELOPMENT, OR CREATION, OF HARMONIES ON ALL KINDS OF
KEYED, WIND, AND STRINGED INSTRUMENTS, INCLUDING THE MOST PERFECT
OF ALL, THE HUMAN VOICE.

"In every art or science, we expect accuracy according to the nature of the subject-matter, and the end
which it is proposed to attain."

THIS scheme is grounded upon the belief that a key has been gained which unites grandeur with simplicity, the laws of which are wonderfully simple, although most complex in their working, explaining all the intricacies which arise in the developments of harmonies.

There is much paradox, and the scheme differs so much from any hitherto published on the subject, that I am aware that, if any link can be found to be wanting in the chain, the defect will immediately be seized upon. I believe, however, that it will be found to admit of clear demonstration. Anyone who has studied the subject knows the difficulties that arise on all sides. In the problem before us, we have to reduce large fields of thought to certain elementary truths. In my endeavour to do this, I have been entirely dependent upon the discovery of the laws of Nature, as my ear is not musical enough to assist me in the matter. "All mysteries are either truths concealing deeper truths, or errors concealing deeper errors," and thus, as the mysteries unfold, truth or error will show itself in a gradually clearer light. The great mystery of music lies in its infinite resources; it teems with subtle elements and strange analogies. A musical note may be compared to a machine: we touch the spring and set the machine in motion, but the complex machinery exists beforehand, quite independent of our will; the motive power is not of our creation, and the laws on which its operation depends are superior to our control. The complex work of harmony is governed by the laws which are originated by the Creator; every note performs what He has willed, and in tracing these laws let us not be indifferent about their Author, but ever bear in mind that the *source* or fountain of the life and activity of harmonies arises from the Power who created the machine, and who knows how it will act. Let us also remember that we understand this machine but partially, and govern it but imperfectly, as indeed the finite can only, in a small measure, grasp the Infinite; and in any

study of the natural sciences, as we progress, we find that "hills peep o'er hills, and alps o'er alps arise." As regards keyed instruments, it appears that the effect of those notes which act two parts, such as C♯ and D♭, is rectified in some way so as to be perfectly attuned to the ideal of harmony within us. Again, the "Amen" sung by the choir in a cathedral may not be in accurate tune, but if nearly the correct intonation is sounded, after travelling along the aisles, the chords always return to the ear in perfect harmony, because the natural laws of music, assisted by the echoing power of the building, have attuned them to the perfect harmonical triad. If the "Amen" be too much out of tune, these laws decline to interfere, and there is no such helpful resonance.* Here we see why music, as a science, takes the priority of painting; for if music is good, it is perfected by natural laws which cause its tones to melt into each other in the most delicate gradations, while the painter who endeavours to represent the exquisite variations of tints and lights in the living landscape is dependent entirely upon his own resources. The early writers on music were philosophers and mathematicians on the broad basis of general science, not on that of music only. Mathematicians, for the most part, have only studied the subject of musical sounds up to a certain point, and have then left it. The musician must take the chromatic scale—not as it exists in Nature, for that offered by the mathematician, without the ordinary compensations of conventional theory, is of no use to the practical musician. Of course, true Art cannot be opposed to Nature, although all the rules of the musician are not the facts of Nature. Music, pure, natural, and harmonical, in the true and evident sense of the term, is the division of any key-note, or starting-point, into its integral and ultimate parts, and the descending divisions will always answer to the ascending, having reference to a general whole. The essence and mystery in the development of harmonies consist in the fact that every key-note, or unit, is a nucleus including the past, the present, and the future, having in itself an inherent power, with a tendency to expand and contract. In the natural system, as each series rises, its contents expand and fall back to the original limit from any point ascending or descending; we cannot perceive finality in any ultimate; every tone is related to higher and lower tones, and must be a part of an organised whole. It is well known how deeply the late Sir John Herschel studied this subject; and it was his opinion that there was some principle in the science of music which had yet to be discovered.

I think it will be seen that most of the difficulties in the rules of harmony arise from not taking the key-note, with the six tones which it developes from itself, as guiding the ear, first to the six notes of its harmony, and then to the key-note which becomes the leader of the scale. In the study of the natural gamut,

---

* See remarks on the wonderful power of the ear in adjusting defects of intonation in Macfarren's *Lectures on Harmony*, No. II.

the artificial system must not be mixed up. The wonders of Nature's laws in the developments of harmonies, consist in the beautiful adaption of keyed and all other musical instruments to a range commensurate with human powers. The chromatic scale of twelve notes (the thirteenth being the octave) is not the scale of Nature. To construct a musical instrument upon real divisions of musical tones, each of them being in correct ratio with the others, it would be necessary to have a larger number of tones to the octave. In the development of harmonies on the natural system, we trace the perfect adaptation of means to ends, meeting the intricacies of every musical instrument, including that most perfect of all— the human voice.

If the laws which I shall endeavour to explain develope the twelve major harmonies, with each note in succession expanding its six tones from within itself; and if each of these is found to be a lower development, which leads the ear to a corresponding higher expansion of the twelve major key-notes, and the six tones of each ascending and descending in an unbroken sequence from any twelve consecutively, the thirteenth being the octave of the first, which commences a higher or a lower series; and if the twelve minor harmonies are also gained by the same laws from their twelve relative key-notes (the thirteenth again being octave): if, again, all other notes are shown to be but higher or lower repetitions of these twenty-four harmonies—may we not consider the problem as in some measure solved? especially as the harmonies proceed in geometric as well as harmonical ratio, and an accurate parallel can be traced between the development of notes and colours, which latter correspond with all the intricacies of harmonic sounds.

In the diagrams the circles are not drawn as interlacing into each other, from the difficulty of representing them accurately as rising spirally in geometric progression. If we endeavour to realise the development of harmonies, both in geometric order, and at the same time advancing and retiring, as in musical clef, we must imagine a musician having the physical power of striking all the notes on a *circular* keyed instrument of seven octaves, linked to a lower series of seven octaves, and a corresponding series of seven higher. But in fact the depth of the lower series, and the height of the higher, are alike unfathomable to our present powers. C, the first note of the seven octaves, sounds the four lowest tones, F, G, A, B of the lower series; and B, the last and highest note of the seven octaves, sounds in its harmony C♯ and D♯ of the higher series of sevens.

CHAPTER III.

ON COLOURS AS DEVELOPED BY THE SAME LAWS AS MUSICAL HARMONIES.

"And God said, Let there be light, and there was light."—GEN. i. 3.
"God is light, and in Him is no darkness at all."—1 JOHN i. 5.

"No Power is save of God, the Powers that be
From Him have being."

WE know not for how many ages colours have been developing. "In the beginning, darkness was upon the face of the deep." The physical properties of light are probably the deepest and most interesting studies in physical science. I only touch upon light as the acting energy or life, causing, in its struggles with darkness, not only the varieties of colour around us, but the colour even of light itself, as colours arise from rays of light exercising different influences.

The primitive laws of any science should be capable of succinct statement, but in combination with others they become more complex and delicate, and error is proved if in the developments they do not echo each other. If, therefore, musical harmonies are correctly gained, the same laws will develope harmonies of colour, and will agree with the colours of the rainbow, the circle of which is divided by the horizon. All who are interested in the laws which regulate these two sciences will doubtless know the interesting lectures delivered by W. F. Barrett (Professor of Experimental Physics in the Royal College of Science, Dublin), and the article written by him and published in the *Quarterly Journal of Science*, January, 1870, entitled "Light and Sound; an examination of their reputed analogy, showing the oneness of colour and music as a physical basis." I will quote shortly from the latter for the benefit of those who may not have met with it. "The question arises, Has all this æsthetic oneness of colour and music any physical foundation, over and above the general analogy we have so far traced between light and sound? We believe the following considerations will show, not only that it has some foundation, but that the analogy is far more wonderful than has hitherto been

suspected. Let us take as our standard of colours the series given by the dis-integration of white light, the so-called spectrum: as our standard of musical notes, let us take the natural or diatonic scale. We may justly compare the two, for the former embraces all possible gradations of simple colours, and the latter a similar gradation of notes of varying pitch. Further, the succession of colours in the spectrum is perfectly harmonious to the eye. Their invariable order is—red, orange, yellow, green, blue, indigo, and violet; any other arrangement of the colours is less enjoyable. Likewise, the succession of notes in the scale is the most agreeable that can be found. The order is—C, D, E, F, G, A, B; any attempt to ascend or descend the entire scale by another order is disagreeable. The order of colours given in the spectrum is exactly the order of luminous wave-lengths, decreasing from red to violet. The order of notes in the scale is also exactly the order of sonorous wave-lengths, decreasing from C to B." "Now comes the important question—Are the intermediate colours of the spectrum produced by vibrations that bear a definite ratio to the vibrations giving rise to the intermediate notes of the scale? According to our knowledge up to this time, apparently not." "Comparing wave-lengths of light with wave-lengths of sound—not, of course, their actual lengths, but the *ratio* of one to the other—the following remarkable correspondence at once comes out:—Assuming the note C to correspond to the colour red, then we find that D exactly corresponds to orange, E to yellow, and F to green. Blue and indigo, being difficult to localise, or even distinguish in the spectrum, they are put together; their mean exactly corresponds to the note G: violet would then correspond to the ratio given by the note A. The colours having now ceased, the ideal position of B and the upper C are calculated from the musical ratio." This quotation on vibrations will be seen to agree with the laws which I have gained. The fact that six of the notes of keyed instruments are obliged to act two parts, must prevent the intermediate notes bearing a definite ratio of vibrations with the intermediate colours of the spectrum. I name the note A as violet, and B ultra-violet, as it seemed to me clearer not to mention the seventh as a colour.

The fountain or life of musical harmonies and colours is E, or yellow; the root B, or ultra-violet: these being, in fact, tints and shades of white and black. Ascending, they partake more of white; descending, of black: the former drawing tones and colours higher, the latter lower.

Throughout the scheme seven tones and seven colours develope in every harmony. In the relationship between tones and colours the seven may be con-

densed into a pair; as an example, we trace the notes and colours in the fundamental scale of C.

C rises from the fountain, and contains all tones within itself.

Red also rises from the fountain, and contains all colours, with white and black.

D = the notes C and E mingled.

Orange, red and yellow mingled.

E = the root of the fountain.

Yellow, containing all colours, is white in its extreme.

F = the notes E and G mingled.

Green = yellow and blue mingled.

G contains all tones.

Blue, with more or less of black and white.

A = G and B mingled.

Violet = blue, and all colours, inclining to black.

B, the key-note of the fountain.

Ultra-violet = violet mingled with more black: a deeper shade of all colours—in its extreme, black.

Notes and colours are thus condensed into a pair springing from the fountain, and mingling with each other in an endless variety. Although yellow as a colour is explained away as white, it is, nevertheless, the colour yellow in endless tints and shades throughout nature, and proves to us that the three great apparent primaries correspond to the tonic chord of the scale of C—*i.e.*, C, E, G = red, yellow, blue; or more correctly, C and G correspond to red and blue with the central fountain of E, white and black mingled, from which all tones and colours arise.

The tones between the seven white notes of keyed instruments, and the tints and shades between the seven colours, cause the multequivalency of colours and of tones; consequently every colour, as every musical harmony, has the capability of ascending or descending, to and fro in circles, or advancing and retiring in musical clef. It is a curious coincidence that Wünsch, nearly one hundred years ago, believed in his discovery of the primary colours to be red, green, and violet; and in this scheme, red, answering to the note C, must necessarily be the first visible colour, followed by green and violet, but these not as primary colours, all colours in turn becoming primaries and secondaries in the development of the various harmonies. To gain facts by experiment, the colours must be exactly according to natural proportions—certain proportions producing white, and others black. In this scheme, green and red are shown to be a complementary pair, and therefore (as Clerk Maxwell has proved) red and green in right proportions would produce yellow. The same fact has been proved in Lord Rayleigh's experiments with the spectroscope. Yellow and ultra-violet,

being also a complementary pair, would produce white, as experimentally proved by Helmholtz.

The development into triplets or trinities has been especially remarked in the harmony caused by the falls of Niagara.* "A remarkable peculiarity in the Arabian system of music is the division of tones into thirds. I have heard Egyptian musicians urge against the European systems of music that they are deficient in the number of sounds. These small and delicate gradations of sound give a peculiar softness to the performances of the Arab musicians.' " Their music is of a style very difficult for foreigners to acquire or imitate, but the children very easily and early attain it. How much the Arabs profited by the works of ancient Greek writers is well known." †

As knowledge increases, may not the beginning of every physical science be traced first as a trinity springing from a trinity in unity, followed by a second partaking of the nature of the first, so as to unite with it in complementary pairs as here described in tones and colours, trinity in unity being the germ of never-ending developments?

The inequality of the equinoctial points is a well-known fact. It will be seen how apparent this is in the developments of harmonies. From the moment that trinities depart from unity, the balance is unequal, and the repeated endeavours after closer union cause a perpetual restlessness. May not this want of equilibrium be the life or *motive power* of the entire universe, with its continuous struggle after concord, even to oneness? "Closer and closer union is the soul of perfect harmony." In tracing harmonies of tones and colours, the double tones of keyed instruments will be seen to correspond with the intermediate tints and shades of colours. The twelve notes, scales, and chords in the major and minor series, the meetings by fifths, &c., all agree so exactly in their mode of development, that if a piece of music is written correctly in colours with the intermediate tints and shades, the experienced musician can, as a rule, detect errors more quickly and surely with the eye than the ear, and the correct eye, even of a non-musical person, may detect technical errors. Although the arithmetical relation has been most useful in gaining the laws, it is not here entered upon; but numbers equally meet all the intricacies both of tones and colours. The bass notes have been omitted, in order to simplify the scheme.

---

* See *Scribner's Monthly Magazine*, No. 81, page 583.   † Lane's *Modern Egyptians*, vol. ii. p. 64.

PART II.

CHAPTER IV.

DIAGRAM I.—THE EIGHTEEN TONES OF KEYED INSTRUMENTS VEERING ROUND, AND
ADVANCING AND RETIRING IN MUSICAL CLEF BELOW—THE TWELVE THAT
DEVELOP PERFECT MAJOR HARMONIES—THE SEVEN WHITE NOTES SHOWN TO
ANSWER TO THE SEVEN COLOURS.

" All, to re-flourish, fades ;
As in a wheel all sinks to re-ascend."

THE five circles represent a musical clef on which the twelve *notes* of a keyed
instrument are written.   Six of the notes are shown to be double, *i.e.*, sounding
two tones, eighteen in all, including E♯, which is only employed in the harmony
of F♯, all others being only higher or lower repetitions.

The twelve which develope twelve major harmonies are written thus ♩, the
other six which are incapabable of developing major harmonies thus ○, without
regard to musical time.   The seven colours are shown to answer to the seven white
notes, the other five being intermediate tones and colours.   A flat marked to a note
indicates that it is nearer to the tone or colour below ; a sharp means that it is
nearer to the tone or colour above.   The notes and chasms are not written
according to accurately measured degrees.

The diagram begins with C, the third space of the treble clef, as being more
convenient to write than C, the lowest note in the bass clef.   The life of musical
sounds rising from a hidden fountain of life is shown by the chasms of keyed
instruments between B and C, and E and F ; their great use will be strikingly
manifest as the developments proceed.   The fundamental key-note C and its root
F rise from the chasms.   B, the twelfth key-note, and E, its root, sound the octave
higher of the fountain B.   The generation of harmonies is by one law a simple
mode of difference.   Each major key-note and its tones embrace the eighteen tones
of keyed instruments which all lie in order for use.   The power and extent of each
are complete in itself, rising and developing, not from any inherent property in
matter, but from the life communicated to matter.   In the whole process of
harmony there are limits, and yet it is illimitable.   Its laws compel each key-note
to follow certain rules within certain bounds ; each separate key-note, being the
fountain of its own system, has its own point of rest, and series after series rise
and enlarge, or fall and diminish infinitely.

CHAPTER V.

DIAGRAM II.—THE TWELVE KEY-NOTES, EACH DEVELOPING ITS SIX TONES IN THE
ORDER IN WHICH THEY SOUND.

"Nature's universal law is progress with self-adaptation."

IN tracing the origin of a harmony, or family of sounds, all divisions must come
out of the one, or *unit*. Two powers are at work—cohesion and separation ; a
truth continually dwelt upon by the Greek philosophers. In the diagram, the note
C may be considered as central, or as placed with four tones below and two
above itself.

A key-note developing its harmony may be compared to a seed striking its
root downwards, and rising upwards. On striking a note, it sounds from within
itself, in a rapid and subdued manner, the six kindred tones necessary to its
harmony, and all which do not belong to that individual harmony are kept under ;
thus all harmonies are in sevens. Each seven forms an ascending and descending
series ; the ear is aware of the tones, but not of the order in which they rise.

The arrangement of a key-note and the six *tones* which it sounds may be
simply explained by writing *tones* in a musical clef as *notes*. In this diagram
we have the harmony of C and its root F. Both of these rise from the chasms,
and hence this harmony is not so closely linked to that of B, and its root E, as to
the other eleven harmonies.

The first trinity of sounds (hereafter called the Primaries) rise veering
from left to right ; the second trinity (hereafter called the Secondaries) follow,
veering from right to left. The life of sound always causes a variety of movement
to and fro.

The three lowest of the six tones are complementary pairs with the key-note
and its two highest tones. Observe the curious order in which the tones sound,
avoiding consecutive fifths. First, we have the key-note and its root, or fellow ;
next A ; then D and its root ; and then E, whose root, A, has already sounded
between the first and the second pair. B, the fourth and central tone in depth,
sounds seventh, and, finding no fellow within the compass of the harmony
developing it, is isolated. Observe also how closely a key-note and its kindred
tones are linked into each other. The Primaries spring from the key-notes, the
Secondaries from the Primaries ; the first pair comprises a key-note and a tone
of the Primaries, the other two pairs have each a tone of the Primaries and a
tone of the Secondaries. The key-note, after giving out its tones in trinities, or

combinations of dissonance, rests, sounding neither scale nor chords. Dissonance does not express opposition or separation, for there is no principle in musical tones which is productive of contraries; the dissonances follow the attraction of the tonic, or key-note, and the neutralisation of the musical disturbance is implied in the disagreement in their motion with the repose of the unit, or key-note. So far is this from producing separation, that the apparent discord is simply a preparation for growth, the life of harmony causing an inherent tendency towards closer union.

We here trace the twelve harmonies developing in succession. Notice how exactly they all agree in their mode of development; also the use of the chasms between E and F, B and C. Remark also the beautiful results from the working of the double tones, especially C♯–D♭, and E♯–F♭, causing the seven tones of each harmony, when ascending, to rise one tone, and, descending, to reverse this movement. F♯–G♭ is the only double tone which acts as F♯ when a key-tone, and G♭ when the root of D♭. The root of each harmony is the sixth and highest tone in each succeeding harmony, rising one octave; when it is a double tone, it sounds according to the necessity of the harmony. The intermediate tones are here coloured, showing gradual modulation. The isolated fourths (sounding sevenths) were the previously developed key-tones; these also alter when they are double tones, according to the necessity of the harmony. Beginning with B, the isolated fourth in the harmony of C, the tones sound the twelve notes of a keyed instrument, E♯ being F♮, and the double tones, some flats, some sharps.

Examine C♯ in musical clef as an example of double tones only developing each one major harmony. C♯ sounds neither B nor E, but C and C♯, F and F♯.

The only exception is the double tone F♯–G♭, which is a curious study. F♯ as a harmony takes the double tones as sharps, and F♯ is E♯. G♭ is also a harmony sounding the same tones, by taking the double tones as flats, and B♮ as C♭. F♯ therefore takes the imperfect tone of E♯, and G♭ the imperfect tone of C♭. (See here the harmony of G♭ in musical clef.)

In the same way are written the two last *primaries* of a series of twelve, which began with C. A higher series of twelve follows, and the first two primaries of a still higher series of twelve. The secondaries are written below the primaries.

We find that on a keyed instrument each primary sounds the same tones as the secondaries of each third harmony below, but in a different order, and the double tones are altered sharp or flat as the harmony requires. For example, the secondaries of B are sharps; when primaries of D♭, they are flats. In order to trace this quickly, the sharps and flats are written to each note.

In any series of twelve, the primaries of the two first key-notes repeat the secondaries of the two last of a lower series of twelve; and the two last secondaries of the twelve in development are sounded as the two first primaries of a higher series of twelve. The three series are thus linked into each other.

CHAPTER VI.

DIAGRAM III.—MAJOR KEY-NOTES DEVELOPING BY SEVENS.

"Creation is the realization of Divine Thought."
"The divine and spiritual are not unnatural, but the very soul of nature." *J. W. Reynolds, M.A.*

THE first circle on this diagram represents seven major key-notes, beginning with C on the third space in the treble clef, and sounding as their roots the seven last key-notes which have developed. The second is a continuation of the first circle. The seven previously developed key-notes are now the roots of seven higher key-notes. The intermediate notes are not coloured, but may be seen to be complementary pairs.

In the musical clef, the sixth and seventh notes from the fundamental key-note C (F and ♯F) are repeated, so that the use of the two poles (♯F and ♭G may be clearly seen, and that the notes and colours precisely agree.

In the progression of harmonies these are always closely linked into each other. If any key-note is taken as central, its root will be the fifth note of its harmony below, and it becomes in its turn the root of the fifth note above. If we add the silent notes, the root of the central note is the eighth below, and becomes the root of the eighth above. To explain the lower series of the notes sounding the six *tones* from within themselves, the only plan appeared to be to write the *tones* as notes in musical clef. By reference to Chapter V., we see that the lowest series still sound their *tones*, and lead the ear to the higher series of a key-note, and the six *notes* of its harmony, as they follow each other in trinities.

CHAPTER VII.

DIAGRAM IV.—THE DEVELOPMENT OF THE TWELVE MAJOR SCALES.

"Oh, how unlike the complex works of man,
Heaven's easy, artless, unencumbered plan!"—*Cowper.*

THE term "key" will now be employed in the ordinary sense of the musician, as a note which keeps all those other notes under subjection which do not belong to its harmony. A good ear requires that the first note struck should govern and regulate the rest, carrying on the intricacies of the key through the seven octaves ascending and descending.

The twelve key-notes, with the six notes of each as they veer round in trinities, are again written in musical clef, and the scales added. The key-note leads the scale, and, after striking the two next highest notes of the seven of the harmony, goes forward, with its four lowest, an octave higher. The seven of each harmony have been traced as the three lowest, thus meeting the three highest in three pairs, the fourth note being isolated. Notwithstanding the curious reversal of the three and four of the scale, the three lowest pair with the three highest, and the fourth with its octave. The four pairs are written at the end of each line, and it will be seen how exactly they all agree in their mode of development. Keys with sharps and keys with flats are all mingled in twelve successive notes. If we strike the twelve scales ascending as they follow each other, each thirteenth note being octave of the first note of the twelve that have developed, and first of the rising series, the seventh time the scales gradually rise into the higher series of seven octaves beyond the power of the instrument. Descending is ascending reversed. After the seven and octave of a scale have been sounded ascending, the ear seems to lead to the descending; but ten notes of any scale may be struck without the necessity of modulation; at the seventh note we find that the eleventh note in the progression of harmonies rises to meet the seventh. For instance, B, the seventh note in the scale of C, must have F♯. This point will be fully entered into when examining the meeting of fifths. To trace the scale of C veering round as an example for all, we may begin with C in Diagram II., and go forward with F, G, A, and B an octave higher. If the twelve scales were traced veering round, they would be found to correspond with the twelve as written in musical clef.

CHAPTER VIII.

DIAGRAM V.—THE CHORDS OF THE TWELVE MAJOR KEYS.

" A threefold cord is not quickly broken."—*Eccles.* iv. 12.
" What is beauty but the aptitude of parts harmonious?"—*Southey.*

ON a keyed instrument only twelve are major key-notes, but as the double tones C♯–D♭ and F♯–G♭ are roots, there are fourteen different chords. The fourteen that are roots are written in musical clef. As an example of the major chords in the different keys, we may examine those in the key of C. A major fifth includes five out of the seven of its key; with the third or central note it is the threefold chord, or fourfold when the octave note is added. Including the silent key-notes, a threefold chord embraces eight, or, counting the double tones, not including E♯, eleven. The first and second chords of the seven of the harmony are perfect major chords in the key of C; the central note of the third chord, being ♯C–♭D, is a discord. The first pair of fifths in the scale, with its central note, is a chord of the key; if we include the octave, the last pair of fifths, with its central note, is the same chord an octave higher than the lowest chord of the seven. Of the chords written in musical clef of the twelve keys, the octave chord is only written to C, the seven of each having two chords and the scale one, thirty-six in all, or forty-eight if the octave chords are added. Notice how the chords of each seven and the chord of its scale are altered.

If the chords of the twelve keys and the thirteenth octave are struck, all agree in their method of development. We see here the order in which the chords are repeated, and the working of the double tones. As an example of the latter, we may trace the chords belonging to the key of D♭, and compare them with those belonging to the key of F♯, also the first chord in the key of A♭. The fourth note in depth, sounded last of the seven of each harmony, has been seen as preparing for the chords; it prepares equally for the scale, and the scale for the chords, the octave chord of the scale, ascending, preparing for the latter to descend. Descending is ascending reversed.

CHAPTER IX.

DIAGRAM VI.—THE TWELVE KEYS RISING SEVEN TIMES THROUGH SEVEN OCTAVES,
AND FALLING BACK AGAIN.

"Painting has been called silent Poetry; Poetry, speaking Painting; and Architecture, frozen Harmony.
The laws of each are convertible into the laws of every other."

IF we strike the twelve keys of harmonies in trinities, scales, and chords, as
written in musical clef, beginning with the lowest C in the bass clef, this
first development is linked into the lower series of seven octaves by the
four lower *tones* sounded by C. If we follow with the twelve *keys six*
times, at the seventh time they will gradually rise into the higher series.
We obtain a glimpse of the beauty arising from musical notes in the
Pendulograph. How exquisite would they be if they could be represented
in their natural coloured tones!—as, for instance, the chord of the scale of
C in red, yellow, and blue, with the six coloured tones rising from each,
and harmoniously blended into each other.

CHAPTER X.

DIAGRAM VII.—THE MODULATING GAMUT OF THE TWELVE KEYS MEETING BY FIFTHS,
ADVANCING OR RETIRING IN MUSICAL CLEF THROUGH SEVEN OCTAVES, AND
VEERING ROUND, ASCENDING AND DESCENDING THROUGH SEVEN CIRCLES.

"What we want is not opinions, but facts, facts, facts."—Laplace.

THE twelve keys have been traced following each other seven times through seven
octaves, the keys mingled, the thirteenth note being the octave, and becoming
first of each rising twelve. Thus developing, the seven notes of each eighth key were
complementary pairs, with the seven notes of each eighth key below, and one series
of the twelve keys may be traced, all meeting in succession, not mingled. When
the notes not required for each of the twelve thus meeting are kept under, the
eighths of the twelve all meet by fifths, and as before, in succession, each key
increases by one sharp, the keys with flats following, each decreasing by one
flat; after this, the octave of the first C would follow and begin a higher series.
It is most interesting to trace the fourths, no longer isolated, but meeting each
other, having risen through the progression of the keys to higher harmonies. In
the seven of C, B is the isolated fourth, meeting F♯, the isolated fourth in the
key of G, and so on. Each ascending key-note becomes the root of the fifth
key-note higher; thus C becomes the root of G, &c.

In the retrogression of harmonies, a key-note and its trinities, by sounding
the same tones as when ascending, leads the ear to the same notes, and the *root*
of each key-note becomes the fifth lower key-note. F, the root of C, becomes
key-note; B♭, the root of F, the next key-note, and so on.

The following table shows the regularity of each seven of the twelve
key-notes ascending by fifths, and the use of the two poles is again seen. The
key-notes and their trinities are closely linked into each other, the three highest
notes of the lower fifth key becoming the three lowest of the higher fifth key,
and the four lowest becoming the four highest in an octave higher. The
twelve keys, rising in each note a tone higher and descending a tone lower,
cause the meetings by fifths. Having examined the table, we may strike the
keys by fifths as written in the musical clef, beginning with the lowest C in

the bass clef, carrying each key-note a fifth higher or descending a fifth lower.
A constant difficulty arises in explaining the development of tones and colours,
from the fact that the *ascending* notes on a keyed instrument are *descending* lines
in musical clef, and the *ascending* lines in musical clef in the retrogression of
fifths must be gained by beginning below and following them upwards. They
are therefore not repeated, either in the table or in musical clef, as descending.

KEY-NOTES.	ROOTS.	FOURTHS.	KEYS WITH SHARPS.		
C	F	B			
G	C	F♯	F		
D	G	C♯	F C		
A	D	G♯	F C G		
E	A	D♯	F C G D		
B	E	A♯	F C G D A	THE TWO POLES.	
F♯	B	E♯	F C G D A E		F C G D A E
C♯–D♭	F♯–G♭	C	G D A E B F♯		G D A E B F♯
A♭	D♭	G	D A E B		
E♭	A♭	D	A E B	KEYS WITH	
B♭	E♭	F	E B	FLATS	
F	B♭	E	B		
C octave					

In the development of the key-notes, the sharp or flat is written to each
note, but not to the keys. The reversal of the three and four notes of each seven
of the twelve key-notes and their trinities meeting by fifths having been traced,
we will now examine the twelve scales meeting by fifths, and the results arising
from the reversal of the three and four notes of each fifth lower scale in the fifth
higher. Take as an example the scale of C: C D E F G A B, and that of G:
G A B C D E F♯. The four lowest notes of the seven of C are the four highest,
an octave higher, in G; F, the central and isolated note of the seven of C, having
risen a tone higher than the octave in the scale of G. The twelve scales thus
modulate into each other by fifths, which sound the same harmonies as the
key-notes and their trinities. Refer to the twelve scales written in musical clef
ascending by fifths, and strike them, beginning at the lowest C in the bass
clef; this scale sounds no intermediate tones, but these must be struck as required
for all the scales to run on in fifths. After striking the seven notes of C, if we
fall back three, and repeat them with the next four notes of the seven; or strike
the seven and octave of C, and fall back four, repeating them and striking the
next four, the four last notes of each scale will be found to be always in the
harmony of the four first of the fifth higher scale. When the twelve scales
ascending have been thus gained, as we trace them also on the table, they may
be struck descending by following them as written in musical clef upwards, and

may be traced in the same way on the table; the third and seventh notes meeting, ascending and descending, sounding one harmony.

SCALES ASCENDING.	3RD NOTES.	7TH NOTES.	KEYS.	THE TWO POLES.
C	E	B		
G	B	F♯	F	
D	F♯	C♯	F C	
A	C♯	G♯	F C G	
E	G♯	D♯	F C G D	
B	D♯	A♯	F C G D A	
F♯	. A♭	E♯	F C G D A E	F C G B♯ D A E sharps
D♭	F	C	G D A E B F♯	G D A C♯ E B F♮ flats
A♭	C	G	D A E B	
E♭	G	D	A E B	
B♭	D	A	E B	
F	A	E	B	

C octave

Finally, trace the twelve keys by fifths as they veer round through the seven circles, each circle representing the eighteen tones. Beginning with C in the innermost circle ascending, C becomes the root of G, G of D, and so on. In descending, begin with C in the outermost circle (though really the first of a higher series which we have not the power of striking on instruments); F, its root, becomes the key-note, B♭ the root and then the key-note, and so on. The keys thus gained are written in musical clef below.

The keys of C and G meeting are coloured, and show the beautiful results of colours arising from gradual progression when meeting by fifths. Each key-note and its trinities have been traced as complete in itself, and all knit into each other, the seven of each rising a tone and developing seven times through seven octaves, the keys mingled. The twelve scales have been traced, developing seven times through seven octaves, all knit into each other and into the key-notes and their trinities. The chords have also been traced, each complete in itself, and all knit into each other and into the key-notes, trinities, and scales. And lastly, one series of the twelve keys, no longer mingled, but modulating into each other, have been traced, closely linked into each other by fifths through seven octaves, three keys always meeting. Mark the number of notes thus linked together, and endeavour to imagine this number of *tones* meeting from the various *notes*.

Three key-notes and their trinities—3 times 7	=	21
Three scales of seven notes each— ,,	7	= 21
Three three-fold chords— ,,	3	= 9
		51

We pass on to the developing of the minor keys.

PART III.

CHAPTER XI.

DIAGRAM VIII.—ON THE DEVELOPMENT OF THE TWELVE MINOR HARMONIES.

"Thou brooding Spirit! Lord and giver of life,
Whose quickening force setteth the quivering pulse
In every living thing."—*Rev. John Andrew.*

THE term "key" in the minor developments must be taken in the sense in which it is understood by musicians, although it will be seen that it is only the seven of the harmony that are the relative minor keys of the majors, the scales with their chords sounding other keys. The grandeur, combined with simplicity, of the laws which develope musical harmonies are strikingly exhibited in the minor keys. Although at first they appear most paradoxical, and, comparing them with the majors, we may almost say contradictory in their laws of development, when they are in some degree understood, the intricacies disappear, and the twelve keys follow each other (with the thirteenth octave), all exactly agreeing in their mode of development. I shall endeavour to trace them as much as possible in the same manner as the majors, the lowest developments of the minor keys being notes with scales and chords, the notes always sounding their major harmonies in tones. Here an apparently paradoxical question arises. If the major keys are gained by the notes sounding the major tones, how are the minor keys obtained? Strictly speaking, there are no *minor* key-notes: the development of a minor harmony is but a mode of succession within the octave, caused by each minor key-note employing the sharps or flats of the fourth major key-note higher; and with this essential difference, it will be seen in how many points the developments of major and minor harmonies agree. I have carefully followed the same laws, and if any capable mind examines the results, I am prepared for severe criticism. I can only express that it was impossible to gain any other results than the seven of the harmony, the ascending and the descending scale and the chords combining three different keys.

Round the circle the eighteen tones of keyed instruments are shown; the twelve developing perfect minor keys are written thus ♩, the seven white-keyed notes are coloured, the intermediate tones left uncoloured.

Probably the lowest harmony which we have the power of partially hearing is A minor, rising in the lower series of seven octaves; C, its highest note, sounding the six *tones* of C, its major harmony, on our horizon of sound. The diagram begins with A, the second space of the treble clef, as most convenient for writing.

Below the circular diagram are seen in musical clef the twelve minor key-notes, as gained from the majors. There is only one meeting of the same note in the seven of every major harmony. All the twelve follow the same plan; the lowest *note* of the seven of C is F, the highest note of the seven is E. The *lowest* tone sounded by E and the *highest* tone sounded by F is the same, A—leading the ear from C to its relative minor A.

CHAPTER XII.

DIAGRAM IX.—THE MINOR KEY-NOTE "A" AND ITS SIX NOTES VEERING ROUND IN
TRINITIES—THE TWELVE KEY-NOTES THUS DEVELOPING WRITTEN IN MUSICAL
CLEF BELOW.

> " Lord, on Thee
> Eternity had its foundations—all
> Spring forth from Thee; of light, joy, harmony
> Sole origin:—all life, all beauty Thine!"—*Sir J. Bowring.*

A S an example of the twenty-four, compare A major, developing, in Diagram II.,
with A minor, Diagram IX., taking the notes in the order which they sound
in trinities. The three notes of the primaries sounded by A minor are, first, the
same root as the major; the two next are the fourth and seventh higher notes (in
the major, the fifth and sixth); the secondaries only vary by the sixth and seventh
notes being a tone lower than in their relative major. Observe the order in which
the pairs unite; the fourth in depth, sounded seventh, isolated. A and its root
do not rise from the chasms. The fundamental key-note C was seen not to be
interfered with, neither is the fundamental minor key-note A; G♯ on the one side,
and B♭ on the other, being the key-notes. The seven of each minor harmony
embrace only seventeen tones. C major and A minor are the only two keys which
sound the seven white notes of keyed instruments. The minor scale and chords
of A are not included in this remark.

When the twelve minor harmonies are traced developing in succession,
we notice how exactly they all agree in their method of development, also the use
of the chasms and the double tones, the seven of each harmony rising a tone
when ascending, but reversing the movement in descending; keys with sharps
and those with flats are mingled. The intermediate tones are here coloured,
showing gradual modulation. D♭ is shown to be an imperfect minor harmony,
and E♭, by employing B as C♭, is seen to be equivalent to D♯.

The primaries, with their secondaries written below each in musical clef,
show that the notes of each primary are the same as the third secondary below,
with the exception that one of the primaries rises a tone higher. The order of
rising varies as in the majors.

CHAPTER XIII.

DIAGRAM X.—MINOR KEY-NOTES DEVELOPING BY SEVENS, VEERING ROUND AND IN
MUSICAL CLEF.

"Life implies this interdependence and harmonious interaction of parts, and the subordination of all to
some universal plan." "Life and intelligence are powers, and rule; but Nature cannot create power,
therefore life and intelligence are from a higher source."—*J. W. Reynolds, M.A.*

IN the first circle are represented seven minor key-notes, beginning with A on
the second space in the treble clef, their roots being the seven last key-notes
that have developed.

The second circle is a continuation of the first; the seven previously
developed key-notes become, as before, the roots of seven higher. The uncoloured
intermediate notes are in the same way complementary pairs.

In the musical clef the sixth and seventh notes from A, the fundamental
minor key-note, are repeated, in order to show the use of the poles D♯–C♭, and
that the colours agree. The use of the two poles, both in the major and minor
series, is strikingly evident.

CHAPTER XIV.

DIAGRAM XI.—THE TWELVE MINOR KEY-NOTES, WITH THE SIX NOTES OF EACH, ARE
AGAIN WRITTEN AS THEY VEER ROUND IN TRINITIES, AND THE SCALES ADDED.

> " Unfaith in aught is want of faith in all.
> It is the little rift within the lute
> That by-and-by will make the music mute,
> And, ever widening, slowly silence all."—*Tennyson.*

THE same laws are followed here as in the development of the major scales.
In that of A, F, the sixth note, has risen to F♯, in order to meet B, which
has previously sounded. In descending, the seventh note, B, falls to B♭, in order
to meet F, which has also previously sounded. The notes, ascending or descending,
always follow the harmony of their key-note, except when rising higher or falling
lower to meet in fifths. We may here trace the twelve, the ascending scale
sounding the fifth harmony higher than its key-note, and, in descending, sounding
the fifth lower harmony. The four pairs of each scale are written at the end
of the lines. If we strike the twelve scales as they follow in succession, the
thirteenth note being the octave of the first, and leader of a higher twelve; having
gained them six times, at the seventh they gradually rise (though beyond the
power of a keyed instrument) into the higher series of seven octaves, and again,
in descending, they fall lower, and are linked into the lower series of seven octaves.
Nine notes of any ascending minor scale may be struck without the necessity
of modulating beyond the fifth harmony. For example, in the scale of A, its
tenth note, C♯, rises to meet the sixth note, which has previously sounded. In
descending, E♭, the eleventh note, meets B♭, the seventh note, which has previously
sounded. The scale of A may be traced veering round by reference to Diagram IX.,
beginning with A, and carrying the four lowest notes an octave higher, F rising
to F♯ in ascending, B falling to B♭ in descending.

CHAPTER XV.

DIAGRAM XII.—THE CHORDS OF THE TWELVE MINOR KEYS.

"No development can help anything which does not have corrective causes working with it; some power must shape the growth, and work correctively by laws impressed and authority maintained. The law of progress must be operated upon and moulded by guiding forces. That which acts, lives; and the universe lives as much by its soul as we do by ours."

> "And what if all of animated nature
> Be but organic harps diversely formed,
> That tremble into thought as o'er them sweeps,
> Plastic and vast, one Intellectual breeze,
> At once the soul of each and God of all?"—*Coleridge.*

> "In all things, in all natures, in the stars
> Of azure heaven, the unenduring clouds,
> In flower and tree, in every pebbly stone
> That paves the brooks, the stationary rocks,
> The moving waters, and the invisible air,
> .   .   .   .   From link to link
> It circulates, the soul of all the worlds."—*Coleridge.*

ALTHOUGH only twelve notes of a keyed instrument develope perfect minor harmonies, there are fifteen different chords, the double tones D♯–E♭, E♯–F♮, A♯–B♭ all sounding as roots. The fifteen roots are written in musical clef. A major and a minor fifth embrace the same number of key-notes, but the division into threefold chords is different. In counting the twelve, a major fifth has four below the third note of its harmony, and three above it; a minor fifth has three below the third note of its harmony, and four above it. A major seventh includes twelve key-notes, a minor seventh only eleven. As an example of the minor chords in the different keys, we may first examine those in the key of A, written in musical clef. The seven of its harmony have two threefold chords, and two of its ascending scale. If we include the octave note, the highest chord of the descending scale is a repetition (sounding an octave higher) of the lowest chord of the seven in its harmony, and the second chord of the descending scale is a repetition of the first chord of its ascending scale. These two repetition chords are only written to the key of A: the chords of the other eleven keys will all be found exactly to agree with those of A in their mode of development. We may again remark on the beautiful effect which would result if the colours of the minor chords could be seen, with the tones, as they develope.

CHAPTER XVI.

DIAGRAM XIII.—THE TWELVE KEY-NOTES, WITH THEIR TRINITIES, SCALES, AND
    CHORDS, THE THIRTEENTH BEING OCTAVE, ARE REPEATED IN MUSICAL CLEF,
    RISING SEVEN TIMES THROUGH SEVEN OCTAVES, AND FALLING AGAIN.

"Religion and science are the two handmaidens of God between whom can be no real variance, because
    they are both divine, both complete, both do the work of their Lord. If they seem at variance, it
    is only because the dull sense of men cannot understand the beautiful variety, yet the heavenly
    harmony of their manifestations."—*Rev. J. W. Reynolds, M.A.*

IF we strike the twelve as written in musical clef, beginning with the lowest
A in the bass clef, each key-note, with its trinities, scale, and chords,
sounds three harmonies. We may follow with the twelve keys as they rise,
and descend by following the keys upwards as written in musical clef, each
key falling lower.

CHAPTER XVII.

DIAGRAM XIV.—THE MODULATING GAMUT OF THE TWELVE MINOR KEYS BY FIFTHS IN
MUSICAL CLEF, AND THE SAME VEERING ROUND THROUGH TWELVE OCTAVES:
THE THREE HARMONIES SOUNDED BY EACH KEY FOLLOWING IN SUCCESSION
THROUGH THE TWELVE KEYS THAT ARE MINGLED AND EVER DEVELOPING.

> "There's not the smallest orb which thou behold'st,
> But in his motion like an angel sings,
> Still quiring to the young-eyed cherubim."—*Shakspere.*

* Observations confirm this: those acquainted with scientific progress must be struck with the fact, that of
late the more brilliant achievements have been made in dealing with the unseen. The microscopist,
the chemist, questioning the ultimate particles of matter; those who occupy themselves with the
mysteries of molecular vibration, bear the victorious wreaths of successful discovery, and show that
every atom teems with wonders not less incomprehensible than those of the vast and bright far-off
suns."—*J. W. Reynolds, M.A.*

BEGINNING with the lowest A in the bass clef, let us strike the trinities, scale,
and chords, carrying each key-note a *fifth* higher, counting the seven belonging
to its harmony. If the silent notes are included, each fifth is the *eighth* meeting.

Let us first examine the meeting of the key-notes and their trinities in
musical clef; the isolated fourths rising through the progression of the twelve
now meet, seven and seven pairing. We must notice how closely they are linked
into each other, the three highest notes of the lower seven being the three lowest
of the higher seven an octave higher, and the four lowest becoming the four highest
an octave higher; we descend by following the keys as written in musical clef
upwards.

We may also examine the table of the twelve tones gained through seven
octaves: the sharp or flat is written to each note, excepting in the keys as they
unite in succession. Each key-note by fifths is seen to become a root of the
fifth higher key-note: thus A becomes the root of E, and so on. In descending,
each root of the fifth lower seven becomes the fifth higher key-note; the key-note
D has G for its root, and so on.

KEY-NOTES.	ROOTS.	2nd NOTES IN DEPTH MEETING THE 6th.		KEYS.	
A	D	E	B		
E	A	B	F♯	F	
B	E	F♯	C♯	F C	
F♯	B	C♯	G♯	F C G	Sharps
C♯	F♯	G♯	D♯	F C G D	
G♯	C♯	D♯	A♯	F C G D A	
D♯	G♯	A♯–B♭	E♯–F♮	F C G D A E	F C G D A E sharps
A♯–B♭	D♯–E♭	F♮	C	G D A E B F♮	G D A E B F♮ flats
F♯	B♭	C	G	D A E B	
C	F	G	D	A E B	Flats
G	C	D	A	E B	
D	G	A	E	B	

A octave

                 TWO POLES.

If we strike the ascending scales as written in musical clef again, beginning with the lowest A in the bass clef, we see that the second and sixth notes of each scale meet in higher harmony; the sharp or flat of the scale which varies from the seven notes of its harmony is written to each note. We descend as written in musical clef upwards; each third and seventh note meet in lower harmony, and thus all exactly agree in their mode of development. Having examined the scales as written in the table below, where the sharp or flat as before is marked to each note, but not to the keys, let us strike the key-notes, trinities, scales, and chords. The three harmonies of each key are written at the end of each line of musical clef. To descend, we follow the musical clef upwards, as before.

ASCENDING SCALES.	2nd NOTES.	6th NOTES.		KEYS.	
A	B	F♯		F	
E	F♯	C♯		F C	
B	C♯	G♯		F C G	Sharps
F♯	G♯	D♯		F C G D	
C♯	D♯	A♯		F C G D A	
G♯	A♯	E♯		F C G D A E	F C G D A E B sharps
D♯	E♯	B♯		F C G D A E B	G D A E B F♮ C♮ flats
B♭	-	C	G	D A E B	
F		G	D	A E B	Flats
C		D	A	E B	
G		A	E	B	
D		E	B		

A octave

            THE TWO POLES.

DESCENDING SCALE.	3rd NOTE.	7th NOTE.	KEYS.	
A	F	B♭	B	
D	B♭	E♭	B E	
G	E♭	A♭	B E A	⎱ Flats
C	A♭	D♭	B E A D	
F	D♭	G♭	B E A D G ⎰	TWO POLES.
B♭	G♭	C♭	B E A D G C	B E A D G C flats
D♯	C♯	B	A D G C F B♮	A D G C F B♭ sharps
G♯	E	A♭	D G C F ⎱	
C♯	A	D	G C F ⎰ Sharps	
F♯	D	G	C F	
B	G	C	F ⎰	
E	C	F		
A octave	F	B♭		

Lastly, we trace the twelve ascending by fifths as they veer round through the seven circles, each circle representing the eighteen tones, beginning with A in the innermost circle. A becomes the root of E, E of B, and so on. In descending, we begin with A in the outermost circle, though it is in fact the commencement of a higher series which we cannot strike. D, its root, becomes the fifth key-note lower, and so on. The keys of A and E are coloured, to show the result of the minor harmonies meeting by fifths.

CHAPTER XVIII.

"Others shall right the wrong,
Finish what I begin,
And all I fail of, win."—*Whittier.*

TO recapitulate from the beginning, observe, firstly, the twelve major key-notes as they have developed from within themselves in succession, six tones in trinities seven times through seven octaves, each thirteenth note being the octave of the first note of the twelve that have developed, and being also the first of the higher series. We may retrace all as still sounding their *tones*, the key-notes leading the ear to the six *notes* of each harmony, the keys with sharps and those with flats being mingled. The ascending and descending scales always agree in their harmonies with the key-notes and their trinities.

Secondly, we have the one series of the twelve keys as they meet by fifths through the seven octaves. The keys are no longer mingled; the scales meet by fifths in the same keys and their trinities.

Thirdly, the twelve minor keys as they develope in succession seven times through seven octaves, always sounding their major harmony in trinities, and, as with the majors, each thirteenth note being the octave of the ·first note of the twelve, and first of the following series, the keys all mingled.

Fourthly, we have one series of the seven of each of the twelve minor keys meeting by fifths through seven octaves. The keys of the twelve ascending scales are written in musical clef above the former, and the keys of. the descending scales below. The ascending scales sound the fifth higher harmonies than the key-notes and their trinities, and the lower scales the fifth harmony lower than the key-notes and their trinities. The three series follow out their keys in three successive series, and all meet by fifths.

The chords always agree in their harmonies, and thus the close union of all is seen. The corresponding harmonies of tones and colours are also shown.

CONCLUSION.

> "Thou art Thyself the secret of Thy works;
> Thou art the key: Thine image bear they all,
> Or more or less. And heaven-born music, as
> Thine ordinance in air and ear, and in
> The balance of the force elastic, with
> The gravitating force that holdeth all,—
> Music the statute is, which more than most,
> Of all that stands on Nature's statute-book,
> Image and superscription—Three in one—
> In interlacing monogram doth show of Thee!"
>
> *Rev. John Andrew.*

THE above quotation from that beautiful work, *The Pendulograph*, shows how firmly its author believes that the Almighty Himself will be proved to be the key to His works; a belief frequently expressed also in a striking work, *Nature and the Supernatural*, by the Rev. J. W. Reynolds, M.A. For many years I have been endeavouring to resolve some of the intricacies of natural harmony with the same views. In the pursuit of knowledge it is eminently important to "avoid profane and vain babblings, and oppositions of science *falsely* so called" (1 Tim. vi. 20), and to remember that facts gained from the study of God's marvellous works, that "ought to be had in remembrance" (Psa. cxi. 4, Prayer Book Version), and the truths of Holy Scripture, can never really oppose each other. Research shows us countless varieties developed by trinities springing from unities, and we find true scientific depth in the Scriptural phrases, where the whole earth is continually mentioned as worshipping the Almighty. This truth is beautifully expressed in the *Te Deum Laudamus*—"Holy, holy, holy, Lord God Almighty; heaven and earth are full of Thy glory."

With our present powers the darkness of ignorance is ever groping after the light of knowledge. If the field is so vast when we merely attempt to harmonise the laws which regulate the visible creation, it widens indefinitely when we attempt to harmonise, by the same laws, Creation with the Scriptures. "God is light," and with His Holy Spirit for our teacher, every line of His word instructs us; "like the ocean, the word remains essentially the same, while the light never plays upon its surface without deepening and varying its hues."

"The real animating power of knowledge fills us with wonder and joy; a joy for which, observe, ignorance is just as necessary as the present knowledge. The man is always happy who is in the presence of something which he cannot know to the full, which he is always going on to know. This is the necessary condition of finite creatures with divinely rooted and divinely directed intelligence; this, therefore, its happy state—but observe, a state not of triumph or joy in what he knows, but of joy rather in the continual discovery of new ignorance, continual self-abasement, continual astonishment."—*Ruskin.*

> "Adore with steadfast unpresuming gaze,
> Him, Nature's essence, mind, and energy."
> *Coleridge.*

> "Speak, ye who best can tell, ye sons of light,
> Angels, for ye behold Him, and with songs
> And choral symphonies, day without night,
> Circle His throne rejoicing; ye in heaven,
> On earth, join all ye creatures, to extol
> Him first, Him last, Him midst, and without end."
> *Milton—Paradise Lost,* Book V.

If we examine the line last quoted by the laws of life which regulate the foregoing scheme, we may compare it with the fundamental threefold chord of the scale of C and its relative colours,　　C　　　　E　　　　G　　　C red rises
　　　　　　　　　　　　　　　　　　　RED.　　YELLOW.　　BLUE.
from the fountain key-note which contains in itself all tones. "Him first," the Son of God proceeding from the Almighty, and yet in Himself the Trinity in Unity. E, yellow or light. E is the root of B, ultra indigo, or black. "Him midst," the Almighty Father, the Fountain of life, light gradually rising and dispelling darkness. G, blue, "Him last," the Holy Spirit, proceeding from the Father and the Son, Trinity in Unity. The Son of God and the Holy Spirit are the complemental working pair throughout the universe; each containing "the seven spirits of life." Red and blue contain all colours in each. C and G are a complemental pair, C rising from the fountain key-note which contains in itself all tones, and C and G combine all tones in each. In Chapter III. it is explained that all varieties of tones and colours may be condensed into this pair, rising from and falling again into the fountain.

If we strike any major threefold chord, and directly afterwards its relative minor, we may notice how they respond to the twofold natures within us of joy and melancholy.

"Joy and melancholy, virtue and vice, are as much the consequences of natural law as the falling of a stone or the growth of a flower."—*C. Watts.*

"Joy and grief are woven fine,
A clothing for the soul divine."

Blake.

"All things are touched with melancholy,
    Born of the secret soul's mistrust
To feel her fair ethereal wings
    Weighed down with vile degraded dust.
There is no music in the life
    That sounds with idiot laughter solely;
There's not a string attuned to mirth,
    But has its chord in melancholy."

Thomas Hood.

The armies of Faith and Science, instead of fighting side by side, too often oppose each other, and as the Archbishop of York remarked in his speech at the last meeting of the Christian Evidence Society, "The undue disposition on the part of Science to come into conflict with Religion, stirs up, on the part of Religion and religious men, a disposition to quarrel with Science." Indeed we all deeply need more solemn feelings of our own littleness, and the greatness of our Almighty Creator.

"Study is like the heaven's glorious sun,
That will not be searched out by saucy looks."

Shakspere.

All the energies of nature are the results of Divine operations flowing from the fountain of life, and all the forces of nature are the forces of life.

"Science has a foundation, and so has Religion: let them unite their foundations, and the basis will be broader, and they will be two compartments of one great fabric reared to the glory of God."—*M'Cosh.*

"Science and Revelation are mutually, though gradually, clearing each other; but as a little warmth of the rising sun only calls up the very mists which are to be dissipated by its more powerful shining, so a vague and chilling popular unbelief is to be dispelled, not by withholding knowledge, but by shedding abroad all possible light. Christianity has one most dangerous mental foe, and that is ignorance." Ignorance is the parent of Atheism; but we should carefully distinguish between "sinful doubt" and candid inquiry, the former of which generally arises from a too great love of, and belief in, our own mental powers.

"Sinful doubts are traitors,
And make us lose the good we oft might win,
By fearing to attempt them."

Shakspere.

"The owlet Atheism,
Sailing on obscure wings across the noon,
Drops his blue fringèd lids and shuts them close,
And, hooting at the glorious sun in heaven,
Cries out, Where is it?"

Coleridge.

I gladly confess that my ruling wish has been to feel my own ignorance deeply, and to trust to the Divine Teacher that my eyes might be opened to see more and more the wonders which may be drawn from the Scriptures, when scientific minds are led to the belief that Creation and Revelation explain each other. As this conviction gains ground, scientific truths will make a more rapid progress, and "the generalisation of Science will no longer be doubtful, but assured."

"Our aim is to promote that agreement by showing the correspondence between truly scientific conclusions and Holy Writ; by making it plain that scientific truths, like spiritual, have for ever been descending from heaven to man."—*J. W. Reynolds, M.A.*

"In Him we live, and move, and have our being."—*Acts* xvii. 28.

Spontaneous life has no existence : whatever is developed below, derives its life from the laws which regulate it from above.

Among the many subjects which excite interest at the present time is the question whether the doctrine of Evolution is true or false. Milton had evidently some glimpse of its truth, as we see in the following lines:—

"Air and ye elements! the eldest birth
Of Nature's womb, that in quaternion run
Perpetual circle, multiform, and mix
And nourish all things; let your ceaseless change
Vary to our great Maker still new praise!"

Paradise Lost, Book V.

If the foregoing harmonies of sound and of colour have been rightly developed from the Scriptures, I trust they will be considered as steps gained towards the belief that Evolution is the law of the Almighty for the continuance of activity throughout the universe, and towards an increasing study of Creation and Revelation as mutually explaining each other. According to my belief, the Scriptures must be based on the principle which is explained of keyed instruments at the conclusion of Chapter II. In the development of musical harmonies the beginning and the ending are unfathomable. It is the same in the Scriptures. No musical note or colour can be separated from those below and above it. Neither can any portion of the Bible be separated : every part embraces the past,

the present, and the future, developing in geometric progression; as the past retires, the future advances. The rests in harmony correspond with silence in the Scriptures, both limiting and illimitable. But there is this essential difference: musical instruments can only be tuned to a certain pitch, whereas the Bible will never need fresh editions or corrections, but as it always has unfolded, it always will unfold, as it is necessary to meet our higher mental powers. I believe that, eventually, scientific minds will arrive at the conclusion that all the energies around us arise from the laws which regulate the life of matter, and cause the continual development of trinities from unities. Continuity everywhere adapts simple laws to wondrous workings. If we evade the belief in the development of trinities, this scheme falls to the ground. We can conceive no grander idea of the power, wisdom, and love of the Parent of the universe than that of His following out His own characteristics, knowing that at any moment, if His life-giving power were withdrawn, all would crumble into dust. Let us link with this thought these glorious promises—

"The grass withereth, the flower fadeth: but the word of our God shall stand for ever."—*Isa*. xl. 8.

"For I am the Lord: I will speak, and the word that I shall speak shall come to pass."—*Ezek*. xii. 25.

"For this cause also thank we God without ceasing, because, when ye received the word of God which ye heard of us, ye received it not as the word of men, but as it is in truth, the word of God, which effectually worketh also in you that believe."—*1 Thess*. ii. 13.

"Whoso despiseth the word shall be destroyed."—*Prov*. xiii. 13.

I have passed so many happy hours in comparing Scripture with Scripture, and drawing from its inexhaustible store the laws which develope the harmonies of sounds and colours, that I feel deep regret in drawing to a conclusion. Throughout the investigation the truth has ever been foremost in my mind—

> "That search and ponder as we may,
>   While onward still we go,
> Till close the night and break the day,
>   We can but dimly know."

T. Davies, M.A.

APPENDIX.

EXTRACTS FROM DR. GAUNTLETT'S LETTERS ADDRESSED TO F. J. HUGHES.

AFTER I had sent this work to the publisher, I looked over letters addressed to me by the late Dr. Gauntlett. They show so much interest in the scheme, that I publish extracts from them.

1867.—"Your plan of eliciting facts from Scripture (altogether new) interests me exceedingly." "To make out the scheme of harmonical parallel proper for the elucidation of your system, it will, if possible, run all true with the harmony of colour, and this has never yet been done, except in a way which has been met with serious objections. When I commenced the examination of your theory, I spent five days at the British Museum, and collated about forty volumes." "I am very glad to hear you have a probability of harmonising numbers by the same laws as light and sound." "What you call rest, I call the appearance and disappearance of a harmonical cycle." "Your series of fifths is quite correct."

1871.—"There has been much written lately respecting colour and tone, but nothing bearing on your own view." "The new theories in music seem inclined to go back to the ancient faith of Pythagoras, everything being used up with the modern notions of tonality. Perhaps we may find a great change at hand; the present system, limiting, as it does, that which is illimitable, cannot be right."

1872.—"It gives me great pleasure to write to you on this subject. Music deals more with the imaginative faculty than any other art or science, and possessing, as it does, the power of affecting life, and making great multitudes feel as *one*, may have more than ordinary sympathy with the laws you work upon. You say 'from E, root of B, the fountain key-note F, root of C, rises.' There is a singular analogy here in the relativities of sounds, as traced by comparing the numbers made together by vibrations of strings with the length of strings themselves, the one is the inverse or the counterchange of the other. The length of B and E are the counterchange of F and C, hence they are twin sounds in harmony."

1873.—"It seems to me, from so many curious coincidences, that truth lies within the system." "I by no means resign the possibility of being able to satisfy myself." "There is no insuperable objection that I can see." "Your theory of the illimitable nature of tones, the limits of six as a one complete and perfect view, and the simplicity of the three pairs, dwell much on my mind. I believe it to be quite new, and in one way or the other quite true."

1874.—"I have been intending to write to you with a full scheme, your scheme so differs from any put forth in these modern days. Like all theories—for there is no exception—my plan does not come up to clear demonstration. It is like the colour theory. No doubt simplicity

of action is the great law, and the same force that excites sensation with the auditory nerve lies at the bottom of sensation with organs of vision. When I say *my plan*, I talk in the old groove, and there are difficulties to be smoothed, but in a way that might be much grumbled over. One very curious thing is plain: your system meets many of the cases on which our present theorists stumble so awfully. I saw this from the first time I had the pleasure of considering it with you, and on this account never relished the idea of giving it up; and the more thought bestowed on it led to its applicability to the more ancient forms of melody—the little tunes of the old world in the East. These are said to be independent of harmony, but your system is perfect harmony. The latest theorists in Paris are all at war with the old theory, and there is now a petition lying before the governing powers of the Paris Academy of Music, praying for a total change in the teaching of harmony in that metropolis; and this memorial has been signed by all the rising celebrities in the musical world there. I really believe the best mode, after all, is the series of six tones—the two trinities; and the law of 'to and fro' is impregnable. That is all right. I should like that term to get into vogue, for it is much more plain and clear than what we call the inverse and reverse, or counterchange." "The grave, or rather extraordinary result of your system is, that so much, very much of it tallies with what may be termed the commonly unknown relatives of the tones. You offer affinities which are termed abstruse, and, although admitted, are accepted without demonstration. Why you should be able to explain the much-quarrelled-over connections is beyond my comprehension, and if I could discover the key, the result would be most important for the well-being of music. With this view your system always interests me. I suspect it lies in that wonderful adaptability of the *order* of numbers. With the artificial system, music is confined to a few single harmonical tones—none of which can ever be used without alteration—which we gently coax the ear into receiving." "Your system runs up the shortest way, and I find it of advantage in composing."

1875.—"It has often struck me that I have never been with you long enough at one time to grasp all your facts, so as to arrange them as a sequence, or set them as a chain. I should very much like to visit you, and hold a parlance upon all knotty points. Just at this moment I am at work on three hymn-books."

The proposed visit was overruled by the sudden death of Dr. Gauntlett in the following February. To show his generous and candid disposition, I may add that, after I had been for some weeks in London, and we had had much conversation, on my writing to him after my return home, asking, "Will you kindly tell me what I owe you for your time?" he replied, "I cannot charge anything, for I often felt, as I walked home, that I had learned more from you than you had from me."

M

FRAGMENTS FROM THE LAST NOTE-BOOK WRITTEN BY DR. GAUNTLETT, DATED JANUARY, 1876.

Dr. Gauntlett's widow has lately lent me for perusal his last note-book, and I feel sure that the extracts from it, which I give verbatim, with her permission, will create interest.

"All theory must be founded on one great fact—harmony; for harmony is the chief beauty of two or more sounds heard together. There may be figure, schemata, and all other niceties of succession and combination; but if no harmony, the music is not beautiful. It is dim, dull, and disagreeable."

"Harmony must be looked at in two ways at least: *first*, up the score from bottom to top—the perpendicular view; *second*, along the score from side to side—the horizontal view. Then as to its periods or pulsations—its to and fro, its flow and ebb. This brings us to rhythm and measure. At the bottom of these lie what is called stress or accent—emission and remission—strong and weak: of these the bar in modern music is an outward and visible sign of certain facts which ought to be in the music, but which, if not in the music, the presence of the bar is of no avail. The bar cannot give stress or accent. 'Wherever there is time, there must be accent;'* but the tick of a clock has no accent. Hullah (or Chorley) should have said life." "The semitone makes music. What operation has it upon the accent or to and fro? It creates the call, it supplies the answer." [This point, I believe, Dr. Gauntlett never alluded to with me, and I have feared that making no difference between tones and semitones might be considered a difficulty with regard to the scheme. In the working of the natural laws of harmony, they must *all* equally be employed.—*F. J. H.*] "Art (grand and true) does not depend upon the teaching of facts. The head is of less importance than the heart. Unless the tone of feeling, the habit and disposition, be well fixed, nothing enduring can come out of the misdirected artist."

"Teaching in song, teaching one another in song and *grace*—a double teaching."

"Beauty in art is not sensual or intellectual; truth, heart-feeling."

"Teach music on some principle. Without a confession of Christianity, this music is mere discipline."

"Teach for some purpose—application, worship; not for pleasure's sake, recreation."

"Church music teaches church doctrine."

"Music worship—habitual exercise of—one of the great occupations of the next life."

Dr. Gauntlett was looking forward to the honour of meeting His Royal Highness the Duke of Edinburgh at the Mansion House, on February 22nd, 1876, regarding the formation of a new English College of Music, and the following notes were evidently the germ of what was passing in his mind on the views which he hoped to express. The reform and elevation of sacred music had been his life-long aim, and he was hoping, under royal sanction, to attain a wider hearing for his opinions. Providence interrupted this plan by his sudden removal from the world the day before the meeting.

"The authorities in the City are interesting themselves in the welfare of the new Musical School at South Kensington. Music is not simply a science, nor is it simply an art; it must be taught on some principle, for some definite purpose." "It must be taught as it was taught in the

---

* See Hullah's Psalter.

schools on the hill of Sion—'out of Sion hath God appeared in perfect beauty.' So long as this principle was recognised in musical academies, there were composers of the highest class; devoid of it, the highest order of compositions disappeared." "Power over music does not depend solely on the mere agreement of 'how to do it.' The student in song will never learn the perfection of beauty except from the preparation of the heart. To make a real musician, there must be a sense of the ever-presence of the Creator of all beauty. The boy-musician must begin his day with prayer, and end it with praise. This made Handel, Bach, Haydn, and Mozart. Music is neither dram nor sweetmeat, neither sensual nor intellectual. It is made so now; but in this order of music there is neither joy nor love, thankfulness nor reverence."

"So long as music was taught primarily for worship, and to proclaim the immortality of man by the inestimable gift of the Royal Ransomer, it culminated to wonders upon wonders." "Noble teachers yield noble teaching, and from such seed the reaping is noble music. To rear the musician with knightly, faithful, and pure feelings, he must believe in his mission and its reward. The law of his life must be the advancement of his art, or rather God's art, given for the honour of the Deity and the elevation of humanity." "The Apostle Paul tells us that we are to teach one another in music, and the greatest doctor in theology, the mightiest defender of the Faith, has been the giant Handel in his oratorio of *The Messiah*. We are told that 'the nineteenth century is weary of the religion of Christ,' and the bright smile of the English boy and the sweet face of the English girl are no longer to be gladdened by the teachings of the holy mystery. The Devil is the strongest opponent to music in its right intention."

I will close this Appendix with a remark once made to me by Dr. Gauntlett. I am sorry I forget where he said it occurred. "After I had been for some time organist, one of the congregation said to me, 'When you first came, the tunes on the organ were loud and clear; now, the voices of the congregation almost drown them.' I replied, 'That has been my aim —it should be so. When I began, the organ was needed to lead the voices: I have been gradually subduing it, that the voices of praise should be uppermost.'"

F. J. H.

The 18 tones of keyed instruments are represented round this circle, and again below in musical clef. As all, with the exception of G♭ and A♯, become in turn either Major or Minor Key-notes, or both, no distinction is made between tones and semitones throughout the scheme. In this diagram the 12 Major Key-notes are written thus ♩ ; the 7 white notes of a keyed instrument are here coloured; the intermediate tones, shown by a flat or a sharp marked to a note, are left uncoloured, being intermediate tints.

DIAGRAM I.

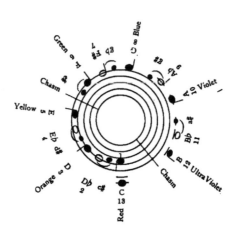

The Major Key-note of C is here shewn developing its trinities from within itself, veering round; C and the other 11 developing their trinities in musical clef. Below each is the order in which the pairs meet, avoiding consecutive fifths. Lastly, C♯ is seen to be an imperfect major harmony; and G♭, with B as C♭, make the same harmony as F♯. The intermediate tones of sharps and flats of the 7 white notes are here coloured in order to shew each harmony, but it must be remembered that they should, strictly, have intermediate tints.

DIAGRAM II.

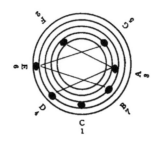

This diagram represents the two last major primaries of a series of 12; 12 of a higher series follow, and the two first of a still higher series: the secondaries are written below the primaries, the sharps or flats belonging to the different harmonies are written to each note. Each primary sounds the same tones as the secondaries of each third harmony below, but in a different order; and the double tones are altered sharp or flat as the harmonies require.

By reference to previous coloured notes it will be seen that all these agree.

DIAGRAM II continued.

The first circle are 7 Key-notes, their roots having been the last 7 Key-notes that have developed.

The second circle is a continuation of the first, shewing the 7 previously developed Key-notes are the roots of the 7 higher Key-notes.

Below, the 6th and 7th Key-notes are repeated, to shew the use of the poles F♯, G♭.

DIAGRAM III.

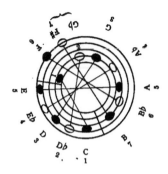

DIAGRAM III continued.

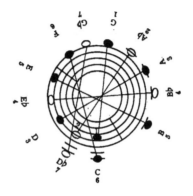

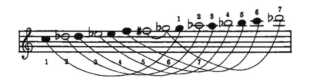

The Sevens of the Key-notes and their scales, the latter written also as they pair by fifths.

DIAGRAM IV.

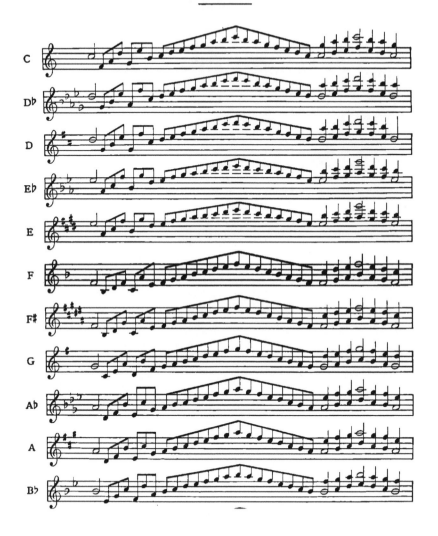

The roots of the chords are first written. The Key-note C and its trinities are shewn to have 2 chords. The chords of the 12 Major Keys, as they follow in order.

DIAGRAM V.

The 12 Key-notes and their trinities and scales written in musical clef, with their chords added, all rising in the two octaves, as before.

DIAGRAM VI.

The 12 Major Keys meeting by fifths through 7 octaves; strike each Key-note, as having risen a fifth higher ascending, and fallen a fifth lower descending.

DIAGRAM VII.

The 12 Major Key-notes meeting by fifths veering round. Each of the seven circles represents a musical clef of the 18 tones. The note or notes, whether in musical clef on spaces or lines, are written here on the circle from which they rise.

Ascending, begin with C in the innermost circle, F being its root. The Key-note C becomes the root of G, G becomes the root of D, and so on. In descending, begin with the octave Key-note C in the outermost circle. F, the root of C, becomes the fifth lower Key-note. F is the next Key-note, and becomes the root of B♭, &c. The 12 Keys in their order are written in musical clef below. Lastly, the Keys of C and G , ascending on a keyed instrument, are written in music as descending; therefore, to shew correctly notes and colours meeting, it is necessary to reverse them, and write C below G. All are seen to be complementary pairs in tones and colours.

DIAGRAM VII continued.

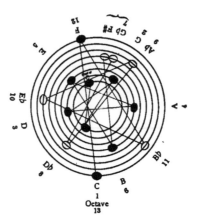

Referring to Diagram I., the 18 tones of keyed instruments are here again represented, both round the circle and in musical clef. In this diagram the 12 Minor Key-notes are written thusσ; the 7 white notes of a keyed instrument are here coloured; the five intermediate tones, as before, are left uncoloured.

The 12 Minor Key-notes, as gained from the 12 Major Key-notes, are written in musical clef.

DIAGRAM VIII.

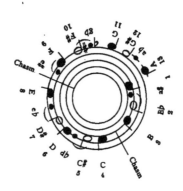

This diagram represents the Minor Key-note A and its 6 *notes* veering round in trinities; A and the other 11 developing their trinities in musical clef. Below each is the order in which the pairs unite, avoiding consecutive fifths. Lastly, D♭ is shewn to be an imperfect minor harmony, and by employing B as C♭, E♭ is seen to be the same harmony as D♯. As before, it should be remembered that the sharp and flat notes should, strictly, have intermediate tints.

DIAGRAM IX.

This diagram shews the two last minor primaries of a series of 12, with the 12 of a higher series, and the two first of a series higher still. As in the diagram of the Major, the secondaries are written below the primaries, and the sharps or flats of each harmony are written to their respective notes. With the exception that one of the primaries rises a tone higher, it will be observed that in the same way the notes of each minor primary are identical with the secondaries of each third harmony below, but in a different order; and the double tones are altered sharp or flat, as before.

DIAGRAM IX continued.

The first circle are 7 Minor Key-notes, their roots having been the last 7 Key-notes that have developed.

The second circle is a continuation of the first, shewing the 7 previously developed Key-notes are the roots of the 7 higher Key-notes.

Below, the D♯ and E♭ are repeated, to shew the use of the two poles.

DIAGRAM X.

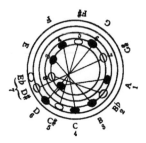

DIAGRAM X continued.

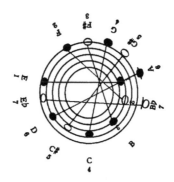

The seven of each harmony, with its scale. Sharps or flats, which vary in the scales from the harmonies, are written to each note, and only govern that one note. The scales are written as they pair.

DIAGRAM XI.

The roots of the Minor Chords. The difference between a Major and a Minor Chord. The chords of the 12 keys follow. The sharps or flats that vary from the seven of the harmony, in the scales written to each note. The last descending chord is here seen to be the same as the first ascending, but this repetitive chord is only written to A.

DIAGRAM XII.

The 12 Key-notes with their trinities and scales repeated, with the addition of the chords 13th octave.

DIAGRAM XIII.

The Minor gamut modulating in the meeting of fifths through 7 octaves. The sharps and flats are written to each note of the scales that vary from the Key of the 7; the Key of each ascending and descending, are also in musical clef at the end of each line.

DIAGRAM XIV.

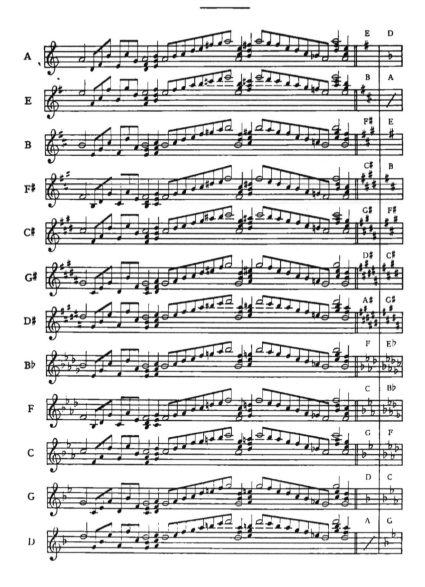

This diagram shews the modulating gamut of the 12 Minor Keys meeting by fifths; each of the 7 circles representing musical clefs of the 18 tones, as before.; the eighth circle being the octave of the first.

Ascending, begin with A in the innermost circle, D being its root. The Key-note A becomes the root of E, E becomes the root of B, and so on. Descending, take the Key-note A in the outermost circle. D, the root of A, becomes the fifth lower Key-note, and G its root, and then G becomes the Key-note, and C its root. The same remarks concerning the writing of the meeting fifths, which are made below the corresponding diagram of the major gamut, apply to this one.

DIAGRAM XIV continued.

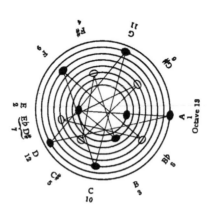

The 12 Major Keys as they rise mingled, with the 13th octave.

· The same no longer mingled, meeting by fifths through 7 octaves.

The 7 of the 12 Minor Keys as they rise mingled, and the 13th octave.

The Key of each 7 meeting by fifths, unmingled.

The Key of the ascending scale written above, and of the descending scale below.

DIAGRAM XV.

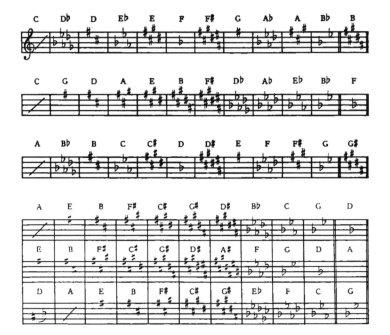

SUPPLEMENT TO

HARMONIES

OF

TONES AND COLOURS

𝔇𝔢𝔳𝔢𝔩𝔬𝔭𝔢𝔡 𝔟𝔶 𝔈𝔳𝔬𝔩𝔲𝔱𝔦𝔬𝔫

BY F. J. HUGHES

𝔏𝔬𝔫𝔡𝔬𝔫:

MARCUS WARD & CO., LIMITED

ORIEL HOUSE, FARRINGDON STREET, E.C.

AND AT BELFAST AND NEW YORK

MDCCCLXXXV.

Supplementary Remarks and Diagrams on the Errors in the Minor Scales as developed by Evolution in "Tones and Colours."

"The Lord is righteous in all His ways, and holy in all His works."—PSA. cxlv. 17. (PSA. xix. 1–4.)

IN preparing for a Supplement to "Tones and Colours," several musicians have carefully investigated the work. I transcribe a copy of Dr. Chalmers Masters' opinion, as he had previously studied colours :—

"I esteem myself fortunate in being introduced to you, and becoming acquainted with your beautiful work on 'Tones and Colours.' I have, to the best of my ability, worked out your idea, by writing down in music the various discords in use amongst musicians, and resolving them according to the laws of Harmony, and I find in all cases the perfect triad agrees with what you term the trinities in colours. The way in which you find the whole circle of Major and Minor keys by pairs in colours is deeply interesting, and *must* be true. The only point of divergence between your system and that recognised by *all* musicians is the *ascending* Minor Scale. No musically trained ear can tolerate the seventh note being a whole tone from the eighth. The Minor second in the lower octave descending is very beautiful, and it is strange how all composers feel a desire to use it. To mention one case out of hundreds, I may cite Rossini's well-known air, 'La Danza.'

"Yours faithfully,

"W. CHALMERS MASTERS."

I was aware that my explanation of the Minor Scales was erroneous. I now see the beautiful Scriptural type which shows how they develope, rising or falling in perfect harmony. I hope to explain this clearly, and I think that any who have doubted my having gained these laws from the Scriptures will then see their mistake.

I had also hoped to write a very brief outline of a few of the innumerable Scriptural types which have guided me in the development of Tones and Colours; but my sight suddenly failed for reading and writing; and I only allude to the seven spirits of God (Rev. iii. 1) as regards tones and colours, and to the twelve fruits of the Tree of Life (Rev. xxii. 2) as regards the twelve notes of keyed instruments.

The Minor Scales are the type of Creation developing, when no Sabbath (or Rest) was required; and we now see this re-echoed throughout the world around us, nothing resting on the Sabbath. A Minor Scale, therefore, cannot sound the

sixth note, which would be Creation perfected, without entering upon the fifth higher key; and it cannot sound the seventh falling into the octave without discord. Therefore the eighth note is not the octave of the first, as it is the fourth note of the fifth higher key.

My first plan was to take away entirely the present development of the Minor Keys; but, on consideration, it seems best to leave them exactly as they are, and to add fresh musical developments of the Minors, explaining them, and leaving it needless, for those who do not wish to look deeper into the subject, to examine the former development. Should they do so, however, they will see that not a single note is altered, the only difference being the Scales developing by fifths instead of by sevenths.

The Major Scales are the type of Creation perfected—man being created, and the Almighty resting—every Major Scale developing the sixth and seventh notes, and the eighth the octave of the first. Therefore, every Major Scale includes the Sabbath, or Rest.

I am quite aware that musicians will set aside the Minors as here written; but I trust *some* minds may be led to examine the beautiful Scriptural types, too deep for our minds ever to find a beginning (the Scriptures have no beginning), and too high for our minds ever to complete ascending.

If, as I believe, the Natural Sciences throughout Creation develope by Trinities, how silently, yet how strikingly, may we trace the wonders of Redeeming Love. "Wisdom hath builded her house; she hath hewn out her *seven* pillars."—Prov. ix. 1. We strikingly see in the development of harmonies the type of 2 Cor. iii. 18, as each key rises from darkness to light, or, descending, falls from light to darkness.

●　　　　　　　　　　　　　　F. J. HUGHES.

BEDWYN LODGE,
SANDOWN, ISLE OF WIGHT,
February, 1885.

Page 13.   *Line* 6. Refer to page 24. Diagram II., F♯ and G♭ are both key-notes, and equally important on keyed instruments.

Page 19.   5 lines from below, add "of" between the words "root" and "B." After the word "harmony" on the last line, add "one always retiring." At the 11th line from below, No. 6 requires explanation. Professor Barrett is not a musician. If F♯, E♯, B♮, and C♭ are included, there are 7 double tones; without these, only 5, viz., the black notes.

Page 20.   After the explanation of the colour blue, add "containing all colours."

Page 27.   *Line* 1. After the words, "major key-notes," add "13 if F♯ and G♭ are both included.
            Line 2. After the word "fourteen," add "to the different chords."

Page 31.   After the note B, G♯, not G♭.

Page 35.   *Line* 3 from bottom, for C♭ read E♭.

Page 42.   *Line* 11. "And" should be "As."

Diagram   *I.*   No. 1 is omitted to the lower C.

Diagram   *II.*   No. 7 is omitted to B, and the key-note is wanting to the harmony of G♭.

Diagram *III.*   In the secondaries of D, A should not be sharp.
(Continued).   Nos. 1 and 2 are omitted to the lower C and D♭.

Diagram   *IV.*   The 3rd note of the trinities of F should be G.

            Line 1. The root F♯ is omitted. It should be coloured green, and F♯ ought not to be coloured.

Diagram   *VI.*   The 3rd note of the trinities of F♯ and F♮ should be G.

Diagram *VII.*   Add to the 4th line of the explanation opposite: "The 8th circle is the octave of the 1st, and beyond our present powers;" and below the remarks that follow, add, "Notice that F♯ is not a root to any major key-note, and how in the growth of keys and the meetings by fifths the use of the double pole is seen, G♭ becoming D♭."

Diagram *XIV.*   Add at the 3rd line, "the 8th circle is the octave of the first."
(Continued).

Diagram *XII.*   For B♯, second line, read B.

On Keyed Instruments as considered Circular.

(Page 17.)

———•———

EXAMINE the notes in the first circular diagrams. Beginning with C, they rise revolving from the right hand to the left; the notes in the musical clef below rise from the left hand to the right, as in keyed instruments. If, however, the volume be turned upside down, the circles will correspond with the music below.

As regards the tones from each note, the primaries rise from the left to the right, the secondaries from the right to the left. This, I believe, as true knowledge is discovered, will be found to be the "to and fro" throughout Nature.

The absence in my mind of scientific knowledge has, I believe, been a great help to me in studying the Scriptures; there is so much apparent contradiction in them. Take one example: "Lord, I believe; help Thou mine unbelief." Do we not feel the truth of this, the two natures thus acting within ourselves?

"Behold! God exalteth by His power: who teacheth like Him"— JOB xxxvi. 22.

ADDITIONAL DIAGRAMS.

The seven of each Harmony, with its Scale. The pairs of the Trinities and Scales.

In the Minor Scale, the Trinities and Scale develope five pairs; the last pair become the fifth higher key-note and its root, consequently the sixth pair would develope the higher key.

The same laws are followed here as in the development of the Major Scales, except that the Minor Scales only develope five notes.

DIAGRAM XVI.

The roots of the Minor Chords. The difference between a Major and a Minor Chord. The Chords of the 12 Minor keys follow.

The student may refer to Diagram XII., where he will find the chords coloured.

Remark the three-fold chord of the Trinity, the highest note is the key-note; and in the three-fold chord of the Scale, the key-note is the lowest note. These are the only two chords in each Minor key.

DIAGRAM XVII.

The twelve key-notes with their Trinities and Scales repeated, with the addition of the chords.

DIAGRAM XVIII.

The Minor Gamut modulating in the meeting of fifths through seven octaves. We may here trace the twelve, each fifth note becoming the higher key-note. But the sixth and seventh notes of the scale are discords. For example, in the key of A, the sixth note, F♮, is a discord with the second note, B♮; and the seventh note cannot be sounded as G♯ falling into the eighth, without being a discord with the third note, C♮. No octave can be sounded in the Minor Scale, as it has risen into the fifth higher key of E.

DIAGRAM XIX.

On Keyed Instruments as considered Circular.

(Page 17.)

E XAMINE the notes in the first circular diagrams. Beginning with C, they rise revolving from the right hand to the left; the notes in the musical clef below rise from the left hand to the right, as in keyed instruments. If, however, the volume be turned upside down, the circles will correspond with the music below.

As regards the tones from each note, the primaries rise from the left to the right, the secondaries from the right to the left. This, I believe, as true knowledge is discovered, will be found to be the "to and fro" throughout Nature.

The absence in my mind of scientific knowledge has, I believe, been a great help to me in studying the Scriptures; there is so much apparent contradiction in them. Take one example: "Lord, I believe; help Thou mine unbelief." Do we not feel the truth of this, the two natures thus acting within ourselves ?

"Behold! God exalteth by His power: who teacheth like Him "— JOB xxxvi. 22.

ADDITIONAL DIAGRAMS.

The seven of each Harmony, with its Scale. The pairs of the Trinities and Scales.

In the Minor Scale, the Trinities and Scale develope five pairs; the last pair become the fifth higher key-note and its root, consequently the sixth pair would develope the higher key.

The same laws are followed here as in the development of the Major Scales, except that the Minor Scales only develope five notes.

DIAGRAM XVI.

The roots of the Minor Chords. The difference between a Major and a Minor Chord. The Chords of the 12 Minor keys follow.

The student may refer to Diagram XII., where he will find the chords coloured.

Remark the three-fold chord of the Trinity, the highest note is the key-note; and in the three-fold chord of the Scale, the key-note is the lowest note. These are the only two chords in each Minor key.

DIAGRAM XVII.

The twelve key-notes with their Trinities and Scales repeated, with the addition of the chords.

DIAGRAM XVIII.

The Minor Gamut modulating in the meeting of fifths through seven octaves. We may here trace the twelve, each fifth note becoming the higher key-note. But the sixth and seventh notes of the scale are discords. For example, in the key of A, the sixth note, F♮, is a discord with the second note, B♮; and the seventh note cannot be sounded as G♯ falling into the eighth, without being a discord with the third note, C♮. No octave can be sounded in the Minor Scale, as it has risen into the fifth higher key of E.

DIAGRAM XIX.

Lightning Source UK Ltd.
Milton Keynes UK
UKHW040705040122
396592UK00004B/367

9 783337 471200